MAKE WAY FOR
DONKEYS

Written by: Janine Jacques

Pictures by: Cheryl Herschleb

Designed by: Ember Co. **www.weareember.com**

Skipper was born with spots. He never quite understood why
his best friend Jasper didn't have any spots. Skipper and Jasper
would run, jump and race all day in fields of green grass and
sleep in a bed of straw at night. Life was good. They were best
friends and very happy.

One day everything changed, the quiet little farm was suddenly bustling with traffic. A big truck backed up to their gate and several men chased them onto a truck.

The truck was crowded and dark. Everyone was very scared. The truck drive for hours then finally stopped.

The doors opened, and everyone was chased into a concrete
pen. There was little to eat, and the water trough was dirty.
Days went by and no one came to see them.

Several of the bigger horses chased them away from the small piles of hay. Skipper and Jasper huddled together against the metal bars of the pen. They were tired, hungry and scared.

Then a miracle happened, a human appeared. She gently stroked Skippers long ear through the bars. It was only for a minute, but it felt so nice, then she was gone. His heart sank and then leaped with joy when she came through the gate with a long rope. She slipped the rope around his neck and led him toward the gate.

Skipper knew that she was going to help him. He followed her on a momentary bliss until he realized she had not put a rope around Jasper. He could not leave Jasper in this awful place, but he knew if he refused to leave with the nice human, he might lose his only chance.

Skipper was not leaving without his friend, so he dug in his heels like a stubborn donkey. He dropped his haunches and spread his front legs defiantly. The nice human stretched her arms and began to pull but immediately realized the problem; this donkey came with a friend. She shrugged, released the rope from Skippers neck and disappeared out the gate.

Skipper adjusted his stance and Jasper slid in beside him. "What are you Crazy? You should have gone with her! If you have a chance, promise me you won't blow it again. Please promise me! You are spotted, little and cute. People will want to take you home. I am just grey." Jasper looked Skipper in the eye and said "Please promise me!" Skipper was silent. His ears hung low.

Suddenly the gate flung open. She was back! Again, the human slipped a rope around Skipper's neck. He could see Jasper slowly backing away. Skipper dug his heels in again defiantly, still he was not leaving without Jasper.

This time however, the kind human had a second rope. She threw it toward Jasper and it looped around his neck. She pulled them both gently toward the gate. The donkeys leaped forward with joy and shuffled through the gate willingly.

They were loaded onto a trailer with fresh straw and hay. They laid down and slept on the long trip to Colorado.

They arrived and were unloaded into a grassy field with fresh
water, a small barn and several other young donkeys. Skipper
did the introductions "Hello everyone. I am Skipper and this
is Jasper."

The other donkeys were curious but not friendly. "Are you runners?" Neither knew what a "runner" was so they answered "No, what is a runner?"

The other donkeys were so nicely groomed and wore pretty colored halters. One answered "We are Pack Racers, actually Santiago over there is the state champion. "

Santiago stepped through the small crowd of donkeys to inspect the new additions. He was bigger than the others, strikingly handsome and stood with his head high. He looked down at the two smaller donkeys and said "Where did you two boys come from? Did they not feed you? You two are just a bag of bones. You'll need to get some food in your belly before you can ever be a Racer."

Skipper and Jasper realized they were unsightly. They had been through a crazy ordeal that had left them skinny, dirty and scarred.

The next day when the kind human fed breakfast to the group. Skipper and Jasper charged in expecting to battle with the others for a morsel of food, but the other donkeys jumped back. Skipper and Jasper dove into the hay pile stuffing their mouths full of green grass hay. They were so hungry.

Later that day, Skipper and Jasper stood together in the corner when Santiago approached. This time Santiago had a kind look in his eye. "Well, you don't have to worry, you'll get plenty to eat here, but you won't make any friends if you charge into breakfast like a bull. We share around here, and I promise you won't go hungry. Rest easy Kiddos this is a good place."

Several days passed. While the other donkeys left each day, Skipper and Jasper stayed in the paddock to eat and sleep. Their ribs slowly began to disappear and what appeared was two handsome little fellas.

Kind humans brushed them and trimmed their hooves. They were given shiny new halters. Skipper's was purple, and Jasper's was blue. Finally, the day came when Skipper and Jasper got to leave the paddock with the other donkeys. They were so excited.

The donkeys were all brought out into the barnyard where a group of humans were making strange poses; leaning over, lunging and stretching.

Then the humans came over and each took the lead of the donkeys and off they all went at a trot. It didn't take long for Skipper and Jasper to figure out the game...it was to run alongside of a human. It seemed a bit strange at first; a human with only 2 legs trotting alongside a donkey with 4, but it was remarkably enjoyable.

The donkeys and humans ran through fields and trails, over bridges and through streams. When it was all finished, Skipper and Jasper couldn't wait to do that again!

And they did. They ran every day. Until one day, they were all loaded up on a trailer. Skipper and Jasper were terrified they were all going back to that horrible place. They shook in fear as the trailer rattled down the highway. Santiago noticed the two boys shaking in the corner and mingled his way through the loose donkeys in the trailer. "You boys are shaking like leaves on a tree - you should not be nervous. Just do your best and go out there and enjoy the race"

"RACE? what's that?" Exclaimed Skipper. "Where are we going?"

"Today is the Leadville Pack Burro Race. It's 15 miles of high country so you Kiddos need to pace your human so they don't wear themselves out get'n out of town. It's rugged terrain but noth'n that you Kiddos can't handle so stop all that shak'n - Race day is supposed to be fun!" Santiago replied.

Just then the doors of the trailer flew open and the festivities began. There were humans, streamers, music and lots of donkeys all lined up.

A loud bang started them all off onto a race course through the dusty hills in Colorado.

After being so scared on the trailer and then so happy to find they were safe and in a race, Skipper and Jasper were full of boundless energy. They ran side by side pulling their humans forward to run faster and faster.

With their heads down and hooves pounding, they made their way past all the other donkeys to the front of the race. The sun was shining, and they were having so much fun!

Fourteen miles flew by and only one mile, and one donkey, remained in front of them. They could see Santiago in the far distance prancing along like a champion.

"We got this" Jasper whispered, but Skipper's enthusiasm was waning. "I can't make it, I need to walk. I am too tired, you go ahead." Skipper said as he started to pull up into a walk.

"Oh no you don't Skipper! I am not leaving you behind!" Said Jasper as he swung in behind Skipper and bit him in the rump. "Get mov'n or I bite you again! I will push you with my head if I have to, but you are not walking!"

Skipper trotted along steadily, and when he started to slow down, Jasper would push him along with his head. It was only a mile, but that mile seemed endless until they saw the finish line ahead and Santiago was only ten feet in front of them!

In a desperate attempt, Jasper reached over and nipped Skipper, which was just enough to push Skipper into the lead. The two dashed forward, past Santiago and just before the finish line Jasper stopped! Only for a second - just enough time for Skipper's nose to cross the finish line before his nose.

Skipper was the winner of the Leadville Pack Burro Race!

Watching Skipper cross the finish line was the second happiest moment in Jasper's young life. He remembered back (two months earlier) to the moment that would forever be his happiest moment. It was on that dark day in that horrible place, when Skipper had risked his life to save his and the human pulled out a second rope to save him too.

EQUINE RESCUE NETWORK

ERN is a nationwide organization dedicated to saving horses, donkeys and mules. We save over 100 donkeys each year that go on to become Pack Burro Racing donkeys, therapy donkeys or barnyard pets. Donkeys are very similar to dogs. They are affectionate, smart and athletic. They have unique personalities and enjoy spending time with humans. The donkeys we rescue arrive in terrible condition; skinny, sick and very scared. Within weeks, these donkeys begin to trust us and start to follow us around like puppies hoping for a treat or a good scratch in those hard to reach places like behind their ears or under their chin. They are hardy little animals that thrive in the woods and on the trails and love to trot alongside their human companions. Since donkeys are so smart, they know we saved them from a horrible fate, and show their appreciation with love and patience for humans of all ages.

While our mission is to save donkeys, we have learned an unintended consequence is that our rescued donkeys make all-sized humans very, very happy.

ABOUT THE AUTHOR

DR. JANINE JACQUES is the founder of the Equine Rescue Network. She is an equine advocate and a strong voice in the plight of unwanted horses and donkeys. She runs regularly with #TeamOlivia in #Massachusetts. #TeamOliva is a group of runners who #Run4Rescue with 8 donkeys and miniature horses.

Janine has authored 2 additional books; "Dogs, Donkeys and Circus Performers" and "Lost Horses". The proceeds of these 2 books have raised over $60,000 for the Equine Rescue Network.

Although, Janine has rescued hundreds of donkeys, rescuing equines is not her fulltime job. Janine has 2 Masters degrees and a Ph.D in Computer Information Systems. Her fulltime job is to manage the Doctoral (DBA) programs at the New England College of Business in Boston, Massachusetts.

ABOUT THE ILLUSTRATOR

CHERYL HERSCHLEB has a Bachelors of Science Degree from Michigan State University and Associates Degree in Nursing from Delta College. She has worked as an Obstetrical/Labor and Delivery Nurse for 33 1/2 years and recently retired. Now living in Traverse City, Michigan, she and her husband have three grown sons, two daughter in laws and three grandsons. She has always enjoyed drawing and painting as a creative outlet. This was her first time illustrating a story. She got involved with this project through her youngest son and his girlfriend who rescued their donkey, Brigs. Brigs now enjoys a good home and burro racing like Skipper and Stuart!

37206928R00024

Made in the USA
Columbia, SC
28 November 2018